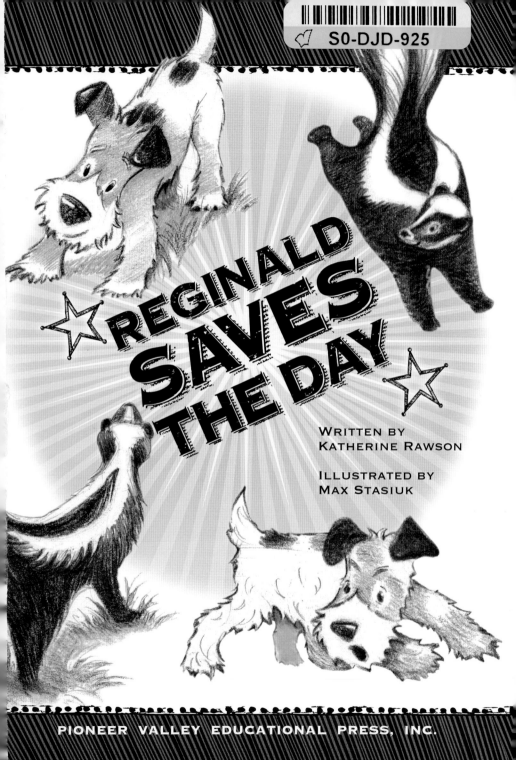

REGINALD SAVES THE DAY

WRITTEN BY
KATHERINE RAWSON

ILLUSTRATED BY
MAX STASIUK

PIONEER VALLEY EDUCATIONAL PRESS, INC.

CONTENTS

CHAPTER 1
NO ONE TO PLAY WITH

Late one afternoon, Reginald was lying on the side porch. Amy and Jack were inside doing their homework. All the other children in the neighborhood were inside doing their homework, too. There was no one for Reginald to play with. There weren't even any squirrels to chase. Reginald was all alone.

Reginald was tired of being alone. He stood up and headed down the street. Maybe he could find some children to play with or some squirrels to chase. He walked down the block, past the neighbors' houses. The yards were all empty. Everyone was inside. Everything was quiet.

Reginald walked for a while, until he came to a busy street full of shops. Things weren't quiet any more. Cars whooshed by and honked their horns. Doors slammed as people got in and out of their cars and hurried down the sidewalk. Everyone was busy. No one noticed Reginald. No one even stopped to scratch his ears.

Reginald kept walking. He went down the block and crossed the street. He turned the corner and saw the park. Reginald ran through the park entrance.

In the park, he saw a squirrel.
"Woof! Woof!" he barked,
racing after it. The squirrel
scrambled up a tall oak tree
and disappeared among the leaves.

Reginald sat under the tree
and looked up into the branches.
He saw a few leaves. He sat
and waited. He sat and waited
some more. Nothing else
happened.

Reginald stood up and looked
around the park. "There have
to be more squirrels here
somewhere," he thought.

Reginald sniffed under bushes and looked up trees. He peered behind rocks. He sniffed all around the playground, too. He couldn't find a single squirrel anywhere.

Then he saw something staring out at him from underneath a lilac bush.

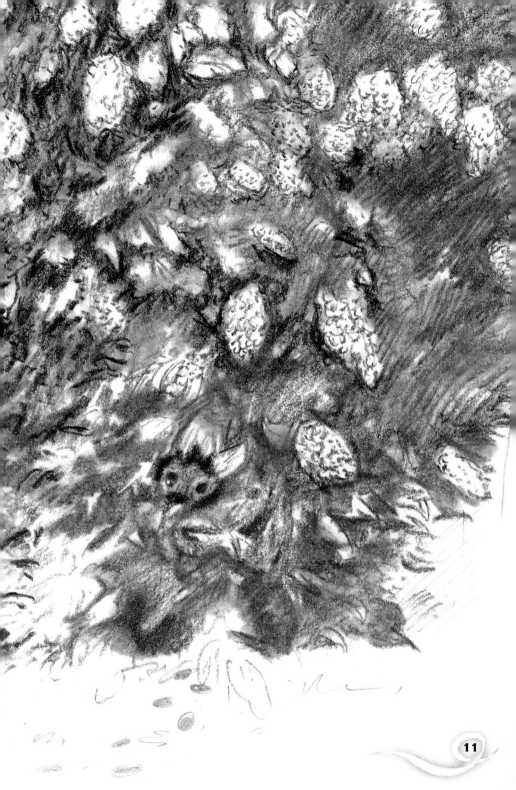

CHAPTER 2
SPRAYED!

Reginald stuck his head under the lilac bush. Two shiny little eyes stared back at him.

"Woof!" greeted Reginald.
He was excited to have someone to play with at last!

The little animal crawled out from under the bush. The animal was covered with black fur. Two white stripes ran down its back and tail.

"Woof! Woof!" barked Reginald again. What he meant was, "Come play with me!"

The little black and white animal didn't want to play. Instead, it turned around, lifted its bushy tail, and sprayed a stinky skunk smell all over Reginald!

"Aroo, Aroo!" howled Reginald. This animal wasn't friendly at all. Reginald turned and raced away, out of the park.

Reginald ran down the street toward home. He thought about the mean thing the black-and-white animal had done. He thought about Amy and Jack. They would scratch his ears and hug him and make him feel better. He ran faster.

Reginald ran past the stores and the busy people on the sidewalk.

"What is that terrible stench?" people cried as Reginald ran past them.

"It's that awful, stinky dog!"

"How disgusting!"

"Yuck!"

When Reginald got to his house, he ran around to the back and scratched at the kitchen door. Then he stood on the step, panting and waiting for Amy and Jack.

"Yuck!" cried Jack when he opened the door. "You stink, Reginald!" Jack slammed the door shut.

Reginald sat down on the step by the door. He was cold. He was tired and lonely. He began to whimper.

He thought about his food dish
and the box of dog biscuits waiting
for him inside. He felt very hungry.
He whimpered a little more.

CHAPTER 3
ON THE PORCH

Inside, Amy and Jack talked
to their parents.

"Poor Reginald is crying!"
said Amy.

"He smells like a skunk!"
Jack added.

"I don't want that stinky dog
in the house!" yelled their mother.

"But he can't stay outside
all night," said Amy.

"He can sleep on the porch,"
their father suggested.

Jack found an old blanket and made a bed for Reginald on the side porch. Amy opened the kitchen door.

"Come on, Reginald," she said, while pinching her nose. "Let's go to the porch." Reginald followed Amy to the side of the house and up the porch steps.

"See? It's a nice, soft bed,"
said Jack as he patted the blanket.

Reginald walked slowly over
to the blanket and turned around
three times.

"Good dog," said Jack, as he
patted Reginald with one hand
and pinched his own nose
with the other.

"Good night, Reginald,"
said Amy.

Amy and Jack went back inside,
shutting the door behind them.
Reginald lay quietly on the blanket.
He could hear his family
inside the house.

"Did you close all the windows
and doors?" asked their father.

"Yes, Dad," said Jack.

"Are you sure? It still smells
a little stinky."

"We closed everything,"
said Amy.

Reginald heard footsteps as his
family climbed the stairs.
He heard doors opening and closing.
He heard water running.
He heard soft voices, saying,
"Good night" and "Sleep tight."

Soon, everyone in the house
was asleep except Reginald.

Reginald stood up, turned around three times, and lay down. After a minute, he stood up and turned around three times in the opposite direction. He lay down again. The blanket was nice, but it just didn't feel right. It didn't feel right because it wasn't his real bed.

Reginald couldn't fall asleep
on the blanket. He sat up
and looked around the porch.
Everything was dark.
He saw the big dark shape
of the table in front of him. He saw
the smaller shape of a chair
next to the window.

Reginald heard the faint sound
of snoring from inside the house.
He realized the window was
slightly open!

CHAPTER 4
THROUGH THE WINDOW

Reginald stuck his head into
the small space between
the window and the sill.
He pushed.
He pushed a little more.

"Squeak!" went the window,
and it moved up a little bit.
There was just enough room
for Reginald!

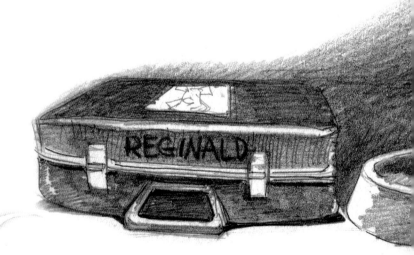

Reginald slipped through
the window and into the house.
He trotted across the living room,
into the kitchen, and right to his
real bed. He turned around three
times and settled down. Then
he closed his eyes and fell into
a deep sleep.

The house was dark and quiet.
Everyone was sleeping now,
even Reginald.

Suddenly, there was a sound.
"Squeak!" went the porch window.
Reginald opened one eye.
"Squeak!" went the window again.
Reginald opened his other eye.
He saw mysterious shadows,
and he heard gruff voices coming
from the living room.

"Quiet!" one of the voices said.

"That wasn't me. That was
the window."

"Shhhh. Do you want to wake
the whole house?"

Reginald saw the beam
of a flashlight sweep
around the living room.

"Look! There's a TV, and those
silver candlesticks look valuable."

"What's that terrible smell?"

"Don't be funny. Help me find
where they keep their money."

"I'm not being funny.
  Don't you smell it?"

"Yeah, it's really stinky.
  Let's find the money
  and get out of here."

Then Reginald heard
  a loud THUMP!

"I told you to keep quiet.
  Stop fooling around."

"I'm not fooling around. I just
  tripped over some kind of ball."

CHAPTER 5
CORNERED

"A ball!" thought Reginald.
He jumped up. Finally,
he had found someone
to play with! Barking loudly,
he rushed into the living room.

Reginald saw a large man
lying facedown in the middle
of the room. A squashed
soccer ball poked out from under
the man's belly. Reginald ran over
to grab the ball.

"Yuck! Stink!" cried the large
man, jumping to his feet.
He rushed to the corner,
where his friend was backed up
against the wall. They both held
their hands over their noses.

"It's disgusting! Let's get out
of here."

"I'm with you. But how?"

The two men looked toward the open window. It was on the other side of the room, and Reginald was standing in front of them with the soccer ball in his mouth. He dropped the ball at their feet and stood back, waiting for one of them to kick it to him.

"Get away, you stinky mutt."

"Shoo! Shoo!"

But Reginald wanted to play. He nudged the ball toward them with his nose, and barked loudly.

Upstairs, doors creaked open.
Footsteps could be heard coming
down the hall.

The two men looked at each other.
Then they glared at Reginald,
who was standing in front of them
with his terrible stink
and the soccer ball.

"Help! Help!" they hollered.
"Save us from this stinky mutt!"

The footsteps pounded down
the stairs. Amy and Jack's parents
ran into the living room, with Amy
and Jack behind them.

"Oh, what a horrible stink!"
they all cried as they covered
their noses with their hands.

"Reginald, how did you
get in here?" asked their father.

"Who are YOU?" cried their mother
as she noticed the two men
cowering in the corner.

"Please, please, save us from this stinky mutt!" cried the large man's friend.

"Call the cops. Call anybody," said the large man. "Just get us away from this stinky mutt!"

"Woof! Woof!" barked Reginald. He nudged the ball toward Jack. "Woof!" he barked again. He felt sad that Jack wouldn't kick the ball.

CHAPTER 6
HERO

Later, the police arrived, and Amy,
Jack, and their parents
all tried to explain
what had happened.
A police officer sat at the kitchen
table taking notes.

"When we came downstairs,"
Jack said, "Reginald had them
trapped in the corner."

"We found our silver candlesticks
in their bag," explained his mother.
"And the porch window was
wide open."

"But they were too scared
to go anywhere," said Amy,
"because of Reginald."

"Where is this brave dog
of yours?" asked the police officer.
"I want to meet him."

"He's out on the porch
eating dog biscuits," said Jack.
"But I don't think you want
to meet him right now."

"He's really stinky," said Amy.
"He smells like a skunk."

"Well, I want you to know your dog is a real hero. The burglars he trapped have been stealing things all over town."

Jack stood up and grinned with pride.

"In fact," the police officer said
"a newspaper reporter
  would like to come over
  in the morning to take his picture."
  He looked toward the window.
"Hey, it's almost morning now."

"Amy and Jack,"
  said their father, "get the garden
  hose and wash that stink
  off Reginald before the reporter
  gets here."

"Use tomato juice," suggested
  the police officer. "A tomato bath
  will get rid of the skunk smell."

An hour later, Reginald, looking
fluffy and smelling sweet,
sat in the front yard.
Amy and Jack and their parents
stood behind him.

"Everybody say *Cheese!*"
said the newspaper reporter.

Click! Flash!

"Wonderful. Now let me get
a photo of Reginald alone.
What a handsome dog!"

Reginald sat proudly on the top step while the reporter got ready to take another picture. Suddenly, the skunk streaked across the yard and into the bushes.

"Woof! Woof!" barked Reginald
as he ran off after the little animal.

"Reginald! No!" cried Jack.

"Come back, Reginald!" Amy called.

But it was already too late.